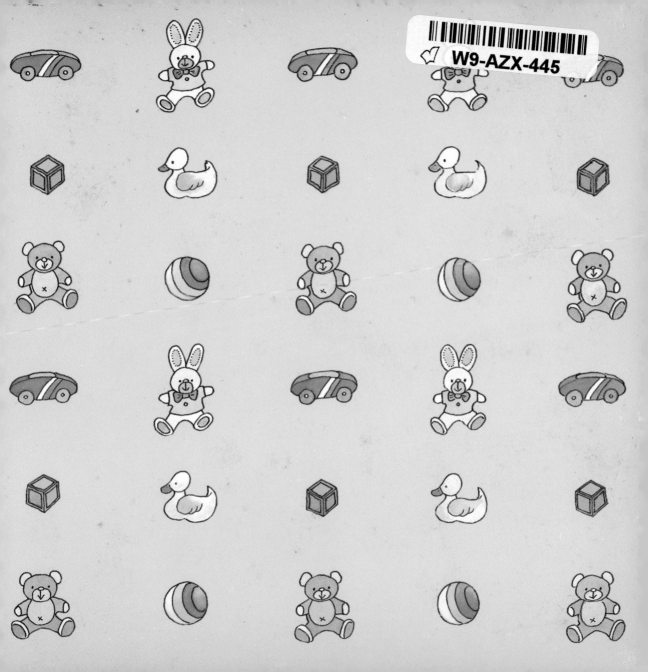

A BEAR IN MY TUB

Written by Judith H. Blau
Illustrated by Barbara Lanza

GROLIER ENTERPRISES INC.
DANBURY, CONNECTICUT

Text © 1991 Judith H. Blau and Nancy Hall, Inc. Illustrations © 1991 Barbara Lanza.
All rights reserved. Printed in the United States of America.
Playskool is a registered trademark of Playskool, Inc. a subsidiary of Hasbro, Inc.
Playskool Bright Beginnings program developed by Judith H. Blau and Nancy Hall, Inc.
Designed by Antler & Baldwin Design Group.
ISBN: 0-7172-8248-1

Scrub, scrub,
There's a bear in my tub.
He's turned on the water.
And now he's jumped in!

He's soapy and sudsy
Right up to his chin.

He's washing his feet.
He's scrubbing his knees.

He's shouting, "More bubbles!
More bubbles, please!"

Scrub, scrub,
There's a bear in my tub.
He's cleaning his hands.
He's rubbing his toes.
He's soaking his tummy
While sponging his nose.

He's wiggling his ears
And swishing his tail.
He's making the boats
All tip while they sail.

Scrub, scrub,
There's a bear in my tub.

Oh! What a mess
He's made with those bubbles.
He'd better clean up,
Or he'll be in trouble.

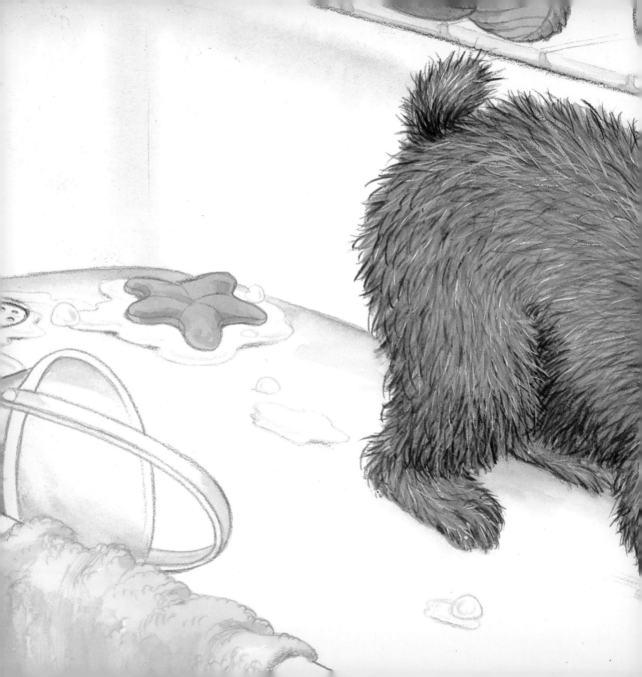

He's pulled out the stopper.
He's rinsing the tub.
He's cleaned up the toys.
He's such a good cub!

He takes down a towel,
So fluffy and soft,
With a shake and a wiggle,
He dries himself off.

This bear is so happy,
Just hear how he laughs.
He has so much fun
When he takes his baths.